Book 7

The Rev Patrick Ashe is a retired vicar who has worked for many years for the cause of children, having been a chaplain for youth and the founder of two relief organisations: Project Vietnam Orphans and Christian Outreach. He has seven children who were the first to hear these stories before they were written down for a wider audience.

By the same author:

Teddy Brown Finds a Home
Teddy Brown is Rescued
Teddy Brown's Secret
Teddy Brown and the Battle
Teddy Brown Goes on Holiday
Teddy Brown and the Aeroplane

Teddy Brown Puts the World Right

PAT ASHE

KINGSWAY PUBLICATIONS
EASTBOURNE

First published 1990

Text illustrations and cover design by John Dillow

British Library Cataloguing in Publication Data

Ashe, Pat
Teddy Brown puts the world right.
I. Title II. Series
823'.914 [J]

ISBN 0-86065-784-1

Printed in Great Britain for
KINGSWAY PUBLICATIONS LTD
1 St Anne's Road, Eastbourne, E Sussex BN21 3UN by
Stanley L. Hunt (Printers) Ltd, Rushden, Northants.
Typeset by Nuprint Ltd, Harpenden, Herts

For Robert
and all the children who listen
to these stories

Contents

A WORD TO PARENTS AND TEACHERS

In this seventh book, Teddy Brown learns about God's secret plan for the world. He also remembers that we celebrate Christmas because it is Jesus' birthday. Pink Rabbit discovers that baptism can be the beginning of a wonderful new life.

At the end of the book there are suggested Bible readings if you should want to get children used to handling a Bible. I recommend using a modern translation such as J. B. Phillips or *The Living Bible*.

1

TEDDY BROWN PUTS THE WORLD RIGHT

Elephant and Toy Soldier were having a stand-up fight in the toy cupboard, and Teddy Brown and Pink Rabbit thought they had better get away and go and see Robby.

Pink Rabbit said, 'I wish they wouldn't fight and quarrel; though I must say it's a lot better than it used to be.'

Just then Toy Soldier came hurtling out of the toy cupboard. It was one of the occasions when he had not come off best, and Elephant had thrown him out. He landed heavily on his back.

'Don't just stand there,' he yelled.

'You're supposed to be Christians—why don't you give me a hand?' They helped Toy Soldier to his feet.

'I tripped over my boot-lace,' he said, and stalked off.

Teddy Brown and Pink Rabbit went into the sitting room where Uncle Harry was listening to the news. It was all about wars and bombs and refugees and hunger. 'My, what a mess the world is in,' he said.

When the news was over, Uncle Harry called out, 'Robby, I'm going to put up a greenhouse in the garden. Would you like to come and help me?' So they all went into the garden.

Uncle Harry and Robby were studying the greenhouse plan, but Teddy Brown and Pink Rabbit wanted to ask questions about the news.

'Why do people quarrel?' asked Teddy Brown, thinking about Elephant and Toy Soldier.

'Because they are selfish,' said Uncle Harry, trying to understand the instructions.

'Why are there wars?' asked Pink Rabbit.

'Because people are greedy,' said Uncle Harry, trying to concentrate on the plan.

'Why do people starve?'.

'Because people don't care enough.' And then he added, 'And I'm going to get this greenhouse into a proper mess if you keep interrupting me.'

'Will it be the same sort of mess the world is in?' asked Teddy Brown.

'It will be, if you don't stop asking questions.'

'I'll get them off your back, Uncle Harry,' said Robby, and turning to them he said, 'Would you two like to do a jigsaw puzzle?'

'Oh, yes please,' they both shouted.

They went back into the house and Robby tried to find a jigsaw for them to do, but all his were too difficult. So he looked in a magazine and found an advertisement for an Airways Company. It had a full-page map of the world, with a little aeroplane in one corner. He took the page out and very carefully tore it into about twenty different shapes. Then he mixed them all up and said, 'There you are; now go and put the world right.'

Teddy Brown and Pink Rabbit went off under the piano and started working on the map. Robby thought, 'That should keep them busy for a couple of days.'

Toy Soldier came up to them. He was still very angry with Elephant, and was looking for someone he could be horrid to. 'What do you two think you are doing? Hatching up some plot, I bet.'

'We're going to put the world right,' said Pink Rabbit.

Toy Soldier snorted. 'Put the world right! Well you'd better start with Elephant—he needs putting right. He's a real rotter.'

Then he saw the bits of paper. 'Oh, you're doing a jigsaw. What is it supposed to be?'

'It's a map of the world,' said Teddy Brown, 'and we are going to put it right.'

'You'll never do that! Why, you don't even know what the world looks like.'

And he walked off.

About twenty minutes later, Teddy Brown came stumping up. 'Come and see, Robby. We've finished.'

Robby could not believe it; but there, all laid out neatly under the piano, was the map of the world.

Robby said, 'How on earth did you manage to do it so quickly?'

'Well, you see, Robby,' said Teddy Brown, 'on the back of the world was a picture of a man—and when we put the man right, the world came right.'

Robby ran out into the garden. 'Uncle Harry,' he shouted, 'I gave them a map of the world to put right, and do you know how they did it?'

When Uncle Harry heard that they had done it by putting the man right, he said, 'That's just how God plans to put the world right. That's what Saint Paul said to some of the first Christians. He said, "God has a secret plan for the world—and the secret is simply this—Christ in you! Yes, Christ in you, bringing with him the hope of all the glorious things to come." You see, Jesus gets men right, and when men get right, then the world will come right.'

Robby said, 'I suppose that is the secret of getting the toy cupboard right. They were a terribly quarrelsome lot before you came, Teddy Brown.'

‘I haven’t done much,’ said Teddy Brown, shaking his head, ‘though it is nice to see the change in some of them.’

‘But don’t forget,’ said Uncle Harry, ‘that each time someone discovers the secret of Christ in you, that is one more on Jesus’ side.’

2

THE BIRTHDAY PARTY

Some people are so busy having fun at Christmas time, that they forget what it is all about. They forget that the parties and the presents, the tree and the turkey, and all the fun of Christmas time is because it is Jesus' birthday.

Many years ago a toy called Chris lived in the toy cupboard. He had not been seen for a long, long time, and only a very few of the toys remembered him. But they often told stories about things Chris had done. Once, when Giraffe was little, he had fallen into the pond, and Chris had risked his life to get him out.

Some of the toys were not interested in the stories about Chris, but a few like Pink Rabbit and Teddy Brown thought he was wonderful, and longed for the day when Chris might come back.

One day, towards the end of the year, Robby said, 'It's Chris' birthday next week; you ought to have a birthday party for him.'

Mr Woollyhead said, 'But Chris isn't here any more. He's probably dead.'

Yusuf, the doll from Persia said, 'Never mind, any excuse for a party.'

So they got crackers and decorations and turkey and pudding and some bottles of fizz, and Toy Soldier got a little bottle of brandy which he hid under the table. They invited toys from other toy cupboards, and Tiger and Dutch Doll thought out lots of games.

When the day came, the guests arrived, and they began to have a tremendous party. It was fantastic—lots of food, games, crackers, paper hats, streamers and lots to drink. Everyone was laughing and talking and having a wonderful time.

There was a knock on the door. Someone opened it, and there was a man doll outside.

'What d'you want?'

'I'm Chris.'

'Oh, really. Well, sorry old man but there's a party going on. Can you call tomorrow?'

And he shut the door.

Chris knocked again. A toy with a big cardboard nose and a paper hat opened the door. 'Well?'

'I'm Chris, the one you are having the birthday party for.'

'Ha, ha, very funny!'

And he shut the door.

Chris knocked again.

Dutch doll opened the door. She looked him up and down and then said, 'Can I help you?'

'I'd like to come in. You see, I'm Chris.'

'Well, I suppose you can come in, but you are hardly dressed for a party. You're in a bit of a mess. Have you had an accident?

You've got blood on your forehead and on your hands.'

But she let Chris in. Everyone was so excited and laughing, that hardly anyone noticed him. Chris went up to Toy Soldier.

'I'm Chris.'

'Oh really—well help yourself to a drink.'

Chris turned away, and saw Golden-haired Doll talking to Yusuf. He said to her, 'I'm Chris.' But she was too busy flirting with Yusuf, and she turned her back on him.

Chris went round and spoke to several others. But no one wanted to know. He sat in a corner and watched.

Then Pink Rabbit heard someone say, 'Have you heard—there's a tramp over there—says he's Chris!'

The other one said, 'Ha, that's good for a laugh!'

Pink Rabbit went to Teddy Brown.

'Teddy Brown, I heard someone say that Chris is here.'

'Chris! Where?'

Teddy Brown ran and found Robby.

'Robby, Pink Rabbit says Chris is here!'

Robby ran to the toy cupboard as fast as he could. He clapped his hands, and there was silence. 'Listen, everybody; I'm told Chris has come back. You know that this party has been given in his honour. I want you all to wish him a very happy birthday.

'Chris,' he called. 'Chris!'

But when they looked for him, Chris had gone.

Christmas is fun, but let's not forget whose birthday party it is.

3

PINK RABBIT LEARNS THAT SHE IS VERY RICH

One day a strange man called at the door, and Robby opened it. The man said, 'Does a little pink rabbit live here?'

'Yes, she does,' said Robby.

'I wonder if I might see her for a few moments?'

'Yes, of course. Come in.'

Robby led him into the play room where Pink Rabbit was sitting by the toy cupboard. Robby introduced her to the stranger, and he was just going out of the room when the man said, 'Oh don't go. As she is your little rabbit now, I would like you to stay.'

Then the man turned to Pink Rabbit and said, 'I'm specially interested in you, Pink Rabbit, because you see, I made you.'

Both Pink Rabbit and Robby looked up surprised. Then the man went on, 'I want to adopt you as a member of my family, and leave you all my savings. But of course, you can go on living here.' And he put his hand in his pocket and pulled out a cheque for a thousand pounds, and handed it to Pink Rabbit.

Pink Rabbit said, 'Oh, thank you—thank you very much.'

Then the man took Robby on one side and said, 'She is a little rabbit without much experience. I want you to help her understand the value of this gift.'

Robby said he would do his best, and the man left.

Pink Rabbit took the cheque and folded it up into a thin strip. She found a loose stitch in her arm and poked it up inside so that it was tucked away safely. Then she went round to the other toys and said, 'I'm

a very wealthy rabbit; my maker has given me a thousand pounds!'

They were all very impressed, and expected her to grow silk fur, but she went on looking just the same. One day, when Pink Rabbit said, 'I'm a very wealthy rabbit,' Teddy Brown screwed up courage and said, 'Well, we haven't noticed any difference, Pink Rabbit.'

So Pink Rabbit went to Robby and said, 'I know I'm a very wealthy rabbit, but I don't really feel any different.'

Then Robby began to explain about cheques. 'That cheque for a thousand pounds your maker gave you is only a bit of paper, but it is worth a thousand pounds because he has signed it. It will make a difference to you when you take it to the bank and cash it.'

Then Robby went on, 'While you keep it tucked away up your sleeve, it's still *worth* a thousand pounds, but it's only a piece of paper.'

'It's a funny thing,' said Pink Rabbit, 'that I can have all this money on me, and yet I'm no better off!'

'Lots of people do that,' said Robby. 'God makes them members of his family, and gives them wonderful presents that could make them happy and content, but they carry them about tucked away, and never use them.'

'Well, I want to use some of my present,' said Pink Rabbit. 'I want to give some of it away.'

So they went down to the bank together, and paid in the cheque, and from then on, whenever Pink Rabbit needed some money, she had a great supply of wealth to draw on.

Robby heard her explaining it all to Teddy Brown one day.

'You see, Teddy Brown,' she was saying, 'I had all that wealth tucked away in my sleeve, and for all the good it was doing me, I might not have had it. Now I've learned how to cash it, and I can use what my maker has given me.'

The following Sunday, Pink Rabbit and Teddy Brown went to church with Robby, and there was a baptism.

'What's happening?' asked Pink Rabbit.

'God is giving that little boy a wonderful gift,' replied Robby. 'He is making him a member of his family.'

'And who are those people with the little boy?' asked Pink Rabbit.

'They are doing what I promised to do for you. They are promising to teach him the value of God's gift and how to use it. They are called "God parents". They are going to pray that one day that little boy will want to accept God's gift, and will want to live as a member of his family.'

'Oh,' said Pink Rabbit. 'Is God's present worth as much as the present my maker gave me? Is it as much as a thousand pounds?'

'It's much more valuable than that. God is surrounding him with his love, and adopting him as his own little boy.'

Pink Rabbit thought about that for a while, and then she asked, 'Robby, now that I have asked Jesus into my heart, am I God's little rabbit, as well as yours?'

'Yes,' said Robby. 'Now we are all members of God's family.'

Teddy Brown said, 'I hope that little boy doesn't do what you did with your maker's gift, Pink Rabbit, and keeps it up his sleeve!'

Pink Rabbit said, 'He's a very wealthy

little boy, though he is too small to know it yet, but some day, when he asks Jesus into his heart, he'll discover it like I did.'

Suggested Bible Readings

1. Teddy Brown Puts the World Right

Luke 11:2.
Colossians 1:26–28.

2. The Birthday Party

Philippians 2:9–11.

3. Pink Rabbit Learns that She Is Very Rich

Galatians 3:26–27.